IT'S NO BIG
DILL!

This book belongs to:

_____

All rights reserved. Published in the United States by Doubleday,

an imprint of Random House Children's Books, a division of Penguin Random House LLC, New York.

Doubleday and the colophon are registered trademarks of Penguin Random House LLC.

Visit us on the Web! rhcbooks.com

Educators and librarians, for a variety of teaching tools, visit us at RHTeachersLibrarians.com

Library of Congress Cataloging-in-Publication Data

Names: Holt, Bob, author, illustrator.

Title: Let's taco about how great you are / by Bob Holt.

Description: First edition. | New York : Doubleday, [2021] | Audience: Ages 4–8. | Summary: "A food-themed,

pun-filled book of advice and encouragement for children" —Provided by publisher.

Identifiers: LCCN 2020010051 (print) | LCCN 2020010052 (ebook)

ISBN 978-0-593-18201-7 (hardcover) | ISBN 978-0-593-18202-4 (library binding) | ISBN 978-0-593-18203-1 (ebook)

Subjects: CYAC: Encouragement—Fiction. | Food—Fiction. | Humorous stories.

Classification: LCC PZ7.1.H6468 Let 2020 (print) | LCC PZ7.1.H6468 (ebook) | DDC [E]—dc23

MANUFACTURED IN CHINA   10 9 8 7 6 5 4 3 2 1   First Edition

Let's Taco about how great you are

Bob Holt

Doubleday Books for Young Readers

HOT DiGGiTY DOG

SOOOOOOO
HaP-

-pea

ditto!

TO KNOW ya!

YOU GUAC MY WORLD!

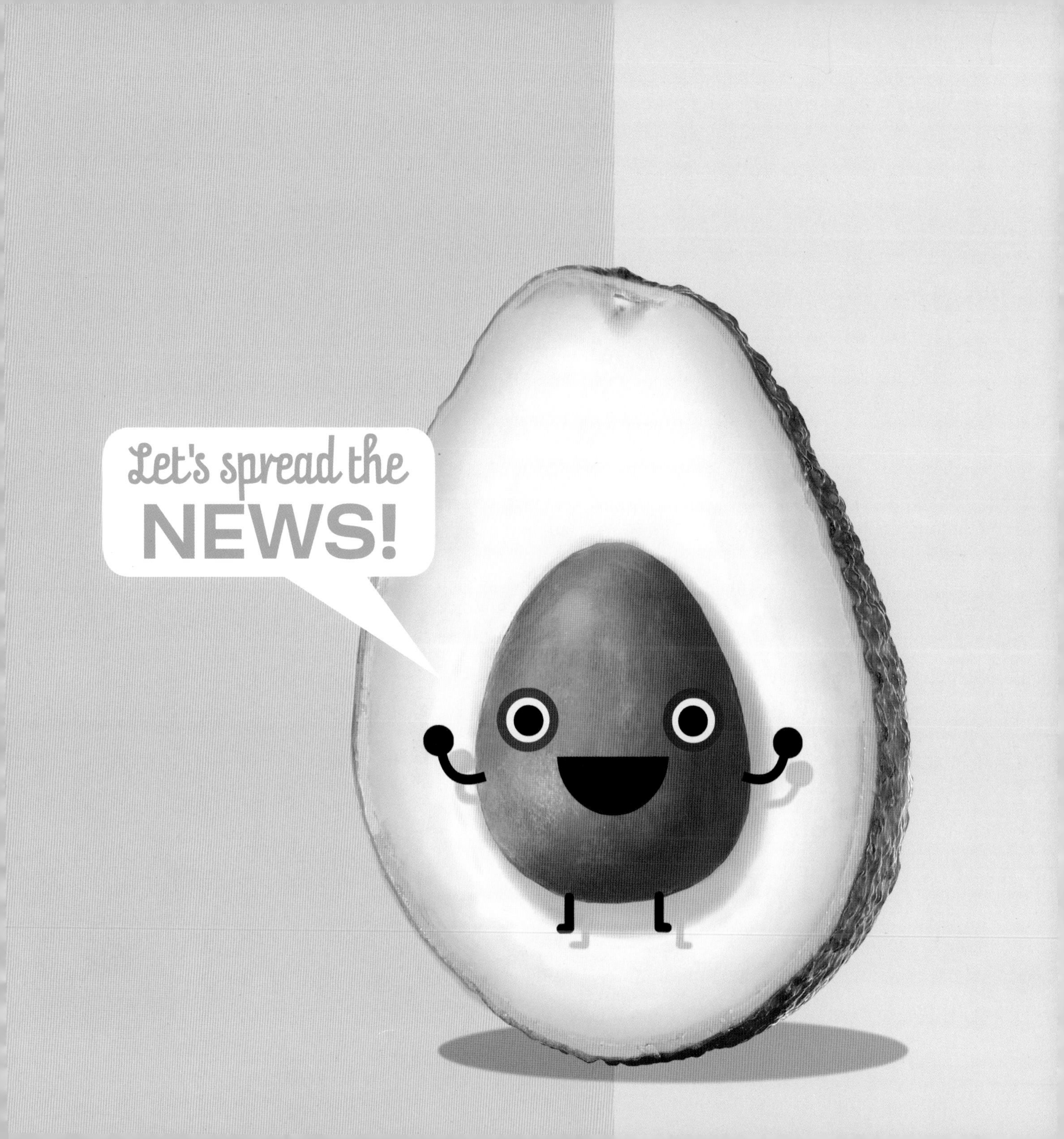
Let's spread the
NEWS!

YOU'RE a smarty pants

AND WE'RE NOT GHERKIN AROUND!

DILL WITH IT

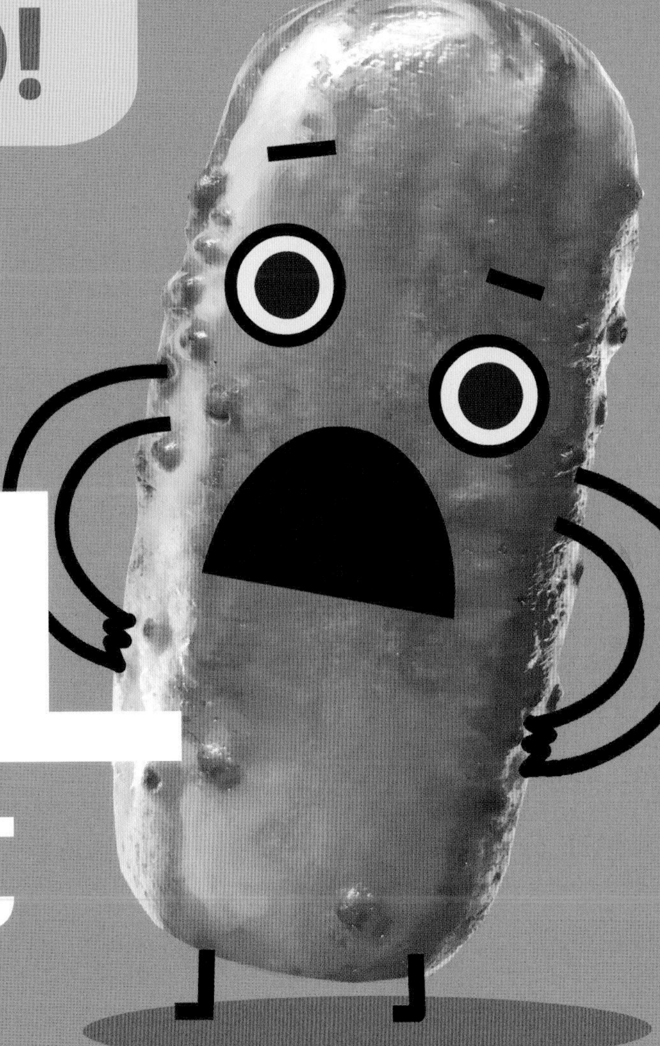

Donut
know how you
do it . . .

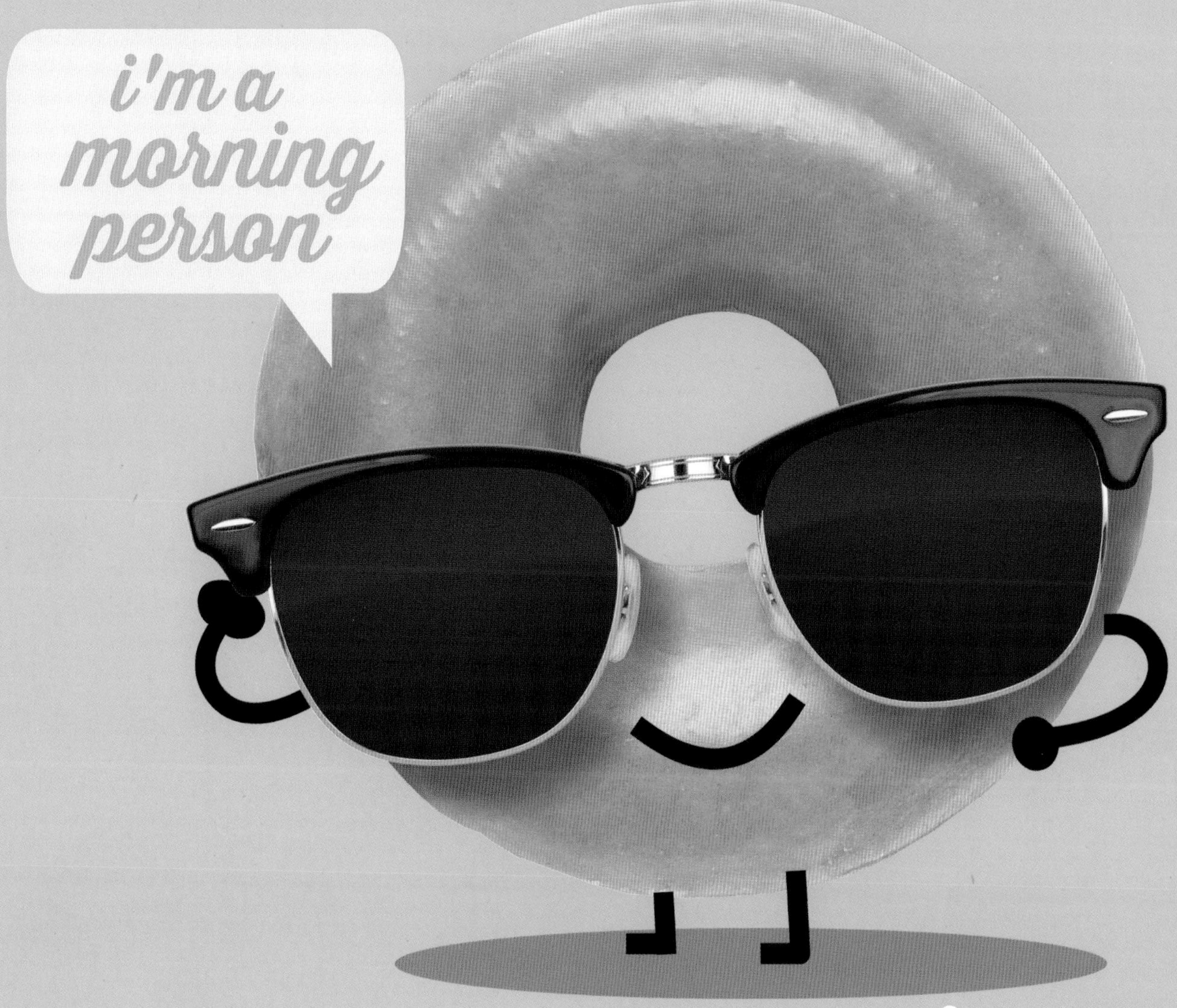

BUT YOU DO IT WITH STYLE

REMEMBER, NOT EVERY DAY WILL BE GRAPE

Monday

Tuesday

Wednesday

Thursday

Friday

Saturday

Sunday

THINGS WON'T ALWAYS GO YOUR WAY. YOU CAN BACON THAT!

Lemme Give you a Few ASPaRaGUS TIPS

DON'T LET
LIFE

PASTA
YOU BY

LIFE is
GOUDA

ALWAYS FIND a
Raisin

SHOULD YOU WORRY?

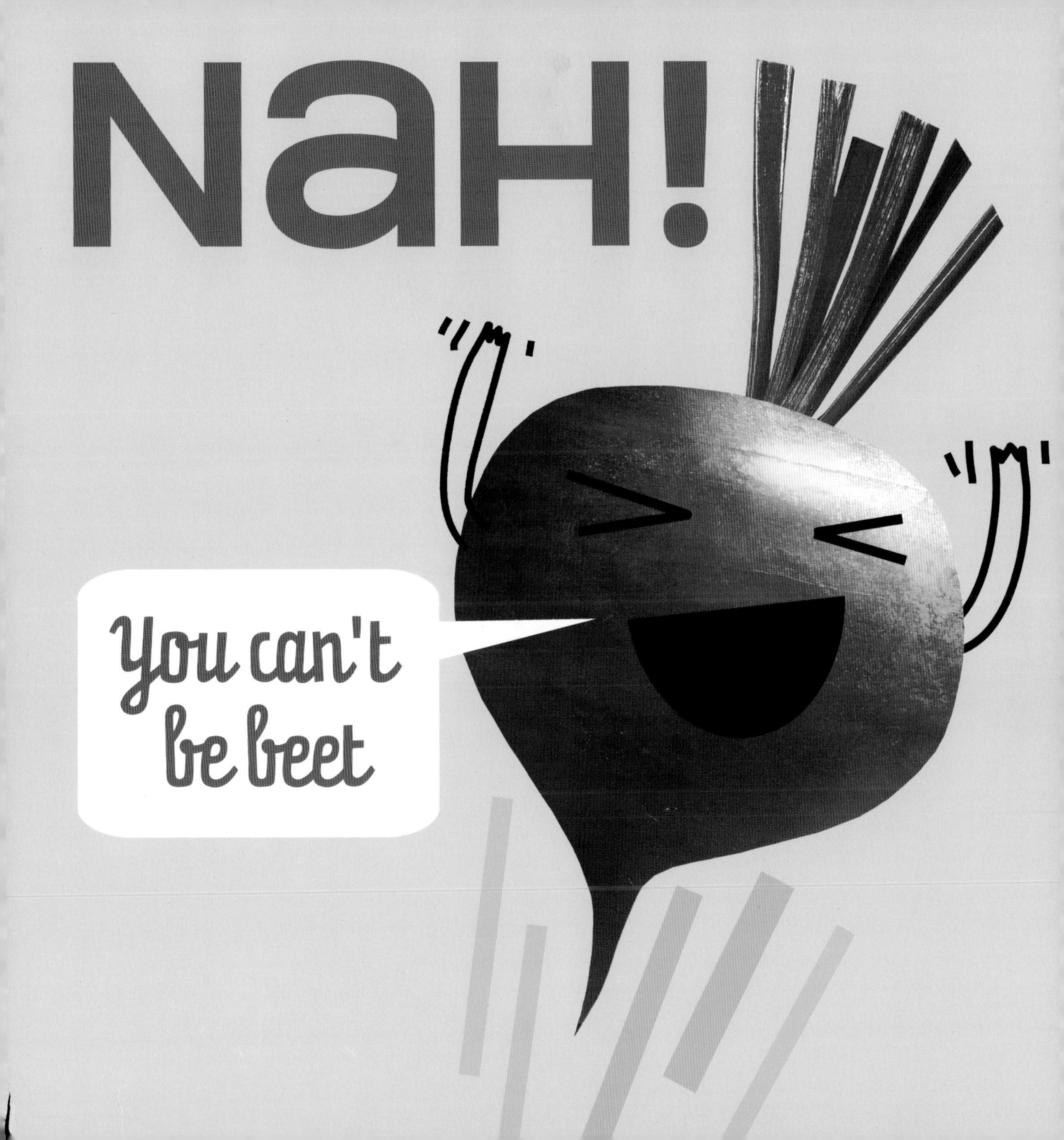
NAH!
You can't be beet

NOBODY KNOWS BUTTER THAN YOU

conquering LIFe's CHaLLenGes can make you FeeL Like...

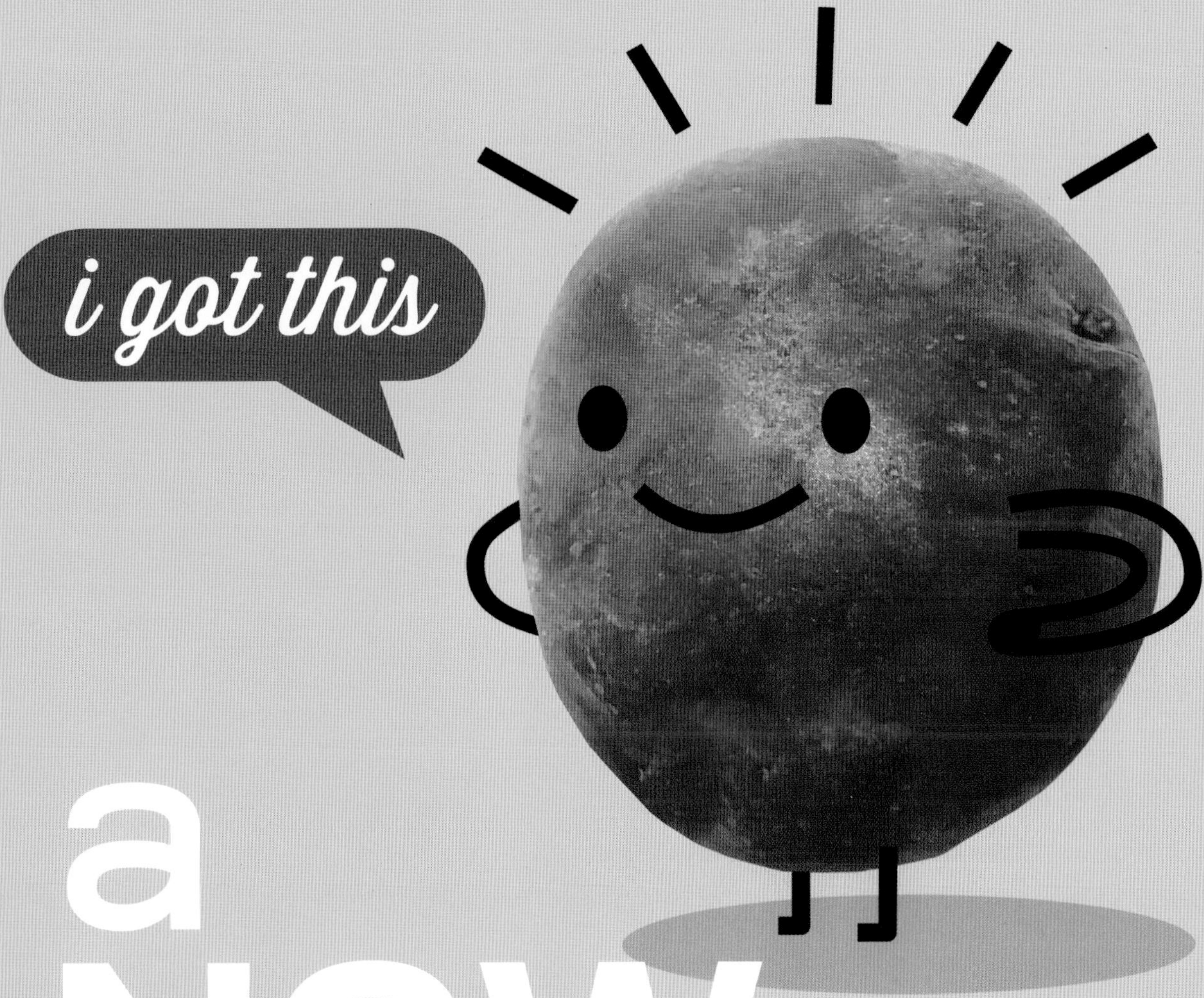

a new potato

IT'S Become apPEARent

so
Lettuce
all
YeLL...